Hey Jack! Books

First American Edition 2012
Kane Miller, A Division of EDC Publishing

Text copyright © 2012 Sally Rippin
Illustration copyright © 2012 Stephanie Spartels
Logo and design copyright © 2012 Hardie Grant Egmont
Design by Stephanie Spartels
Typesetting by Michaela Stone
First published in Australia in 2012 by Hardie Grant Egmont

For information contact:
Kane Miller, A Division of EDC Publishing
P.O. Box 470663
Tulsa, OK 74147-0663
www.kanemiller.com
www.edcpub.com
www.usbornebooksandmore.com

Library of Congress Control Number: 2012931652

Printed and bound in the United States of America
7 8 9 10
ISBN: 978-1-61067-121-7

The Crazy Cousins

By Sally Rippin

Illustrated by Stephanie Spartels

Kane Miller
A DIVISION OF EDC PUBLISHING

Chapter One

This is Jack. Today Jack
is in a moochy mood.
When he is in a moochy
mood, Jack likes to play
all by himself.

Jack is playing with his Lego. He has built an enormous castle with a moat. Now he must save all the people in the castle from the **fierce** dragon.

Jack's dad knocks on the door. "Hey, Jack," he says.

"Don't forget that your cousins are coming over today. You had better get dressed!"

Jack sits up. His cousins? Oh no! He *had* forgotten!

Jack has the noisiest, **messiest** cousins in the whole world.

4

He is *definitely* not in the mood for his cousins today.

5

6

Jack **frowns**.

"Do they have to come?" he asks his dad. "Last time David broke my remote control car. Stella drew on my math book. And Ivy picked all Mom's flowers!"

Jack's dad smiles. "They're your cousins, Jack."

"And we don't see them often," his dad adds. "You'll have to try to get along. Why don't you invite Billie over too?"

Billie is Jack's best friend. She lives next door.

"Good idea," says Jack. He pulls on some clothes and runs downstairs.

But then he remembers.
Billie said she was going
to play at Rebecca's
house today.

Oh no! Three annoying
cousins and no best friend.
What a **disaster**.

Jack's tummy begins to
jump around like a frog.
Soon it starts to hurt.

9

Jack creeps upstairs
and crawls into bed.
He pulls the blanket
up over his head.
All he wanted was
a quiet, moochy day.
Now the noisiest,
craziest cousins
ever are on their
way over.

Jack lies in bed
and imagines all
the **terrible**
things they will get
up to this time.

13

Chapter Two

Soon, Jack's dad
knocks on the door.
"Jack?" he calls softly.
"Come on. Your cousins
have arrived!"

"Tell them I'm not here,"
Jack says from under
the blanket.

Jack's dad comes into the
room. He sits down on
the end of the bed.

"They're here to see you, Jack," he says.

Jack sighs. Then he kicks off the blanket and follows his dad downstairs.

In the kitchen, Jack's uncle and aunt are talking with his mom. Suddenly they hear a **scream**.

16

Everyone looks outside.
David is chasing Stella
and Ivy with a stick.

"David!" calls Jack's
Uncle Bob.

"That's enough!"
Auntie Bee calls.

But Jack's cousins
don't listen. They run
around the garden
like little monsters.

18

Jack sighs. Why does he have to play with his annoying cousins? They are the worst cousins in the world!

He walks outside and sits down on the back step. He wishes Billie was here to help him.

A best friend always
makes things better.

"Hey, Jack!" David calls.
"Do you want to
play soccer?"

"No," says Jack grumpily.
"Last time you kicked my
soccer ball over the fence!"

"How about we make a
potion then?" says Ivy.
"Remember we made
one last time?"

21

"We got in **trouble** because you picked all Mom's flowers," Jack says, frowning. "I don't want to make a potion again."

"I'm sorry," says Ivy in a little voice. She flops down on the back step beside Jack.

David kicks a pebble and Stella chews her fingernails. The three of them look miserable.

"We just want to play with you," Stella says to Jack.

"You're the one with all the good ideas," David says.

"Yeah, Jack!" Ivy says. "You're the bestest, **funnest** cousin in the whole wide world."

Jack looks up at his cousins in surprise.

24

The best cousin?
He didn't know
they thought that!

Jack gets a warm, honey feeling in his tummy. Now he feels bad for acting so **grumpy**.

He certainly hasn't been the best cousin today. He's been the *worst* cousin!

"Well," he says slowly, "I guess you could come and look at my Lego castle."

"Really?" says David.

Jack grins. "It's got a tower and a moat and even a drawbridge!"

"Cool!" shout Stella
and Ivy together.

Jack smiles, and the four
of them run upstairs
to his bedroom.

Chapter Three

When Jack's cousins see his castle, they all gasp.

"Wow!" says David.

"That's so cool!" says Stella.

Jack feels very proud.

"Can we play with it?"

Ivy says, jumping

up and down in

excitement.

"Ummm…" says Jack.
His tummy starts to
wriggle around again.

He doesn't want his
cousins to touch his
Lego castle in case
they break it. But he
doesn't want to be
mean either. Jack doesn't
know what to do.

"Um, all right," says Jack. "But be careful."

"Can I be the knight?" David says.

"Can I be the princess?" Stella says.

"Can I be the dragon?" Ivy shouts.

She picks up the dragon and **SWOOPS** it towards the castle tower.

"Oh no!" says Jack.

But it's too late.

Ivy crashes the dragon
into the tower, and
all the little pieces of
Lego tumble down
to the ground.

David and Stella freeze.
Their eyes grow wide
in fright.

Little Ivy covers her
face in her hands and
begins to cry.

"I'm sorry!" she says.

"I didn't mean to break your castle, Jack."

Jack looks at Ivy. He looks at David and Stella too. He remembers what they said to him outside, and the big, moochy, grumpy bubble inside him **pops**. He smiles.

"That's OK, Ivy," he says.

"It was an accident.

Anyway, Lego is *meant*

to be broken. Look!"

Jack picks up another
dragon and crashes
it into the wall of
the castle. The wall
breaks into tiny pieces.
Jack's cousins look
nervous.

Jack giggles. Then he
crashes his
dragon into the
other wall.

Another part of
the castle comes
tumbling down.

"Come on!" says Jack, laughing. "You can break the rest, Ivy."

Ivy crashes her dragon into the last wall.

The castle is now in **ruins**. Little Lego pieces lie everywhere.

"What now?" says David. He still looks worried.

"Well, now we build
it again, of course!"
Jack laughs.

So Jack and his
cousins build another
castle, taller than
the last one. This time
it is Stella's turn to
crash it down.
Stella and Ivy and
David laugh loudly.

41

42

Jack laughs the **loudest** of all.

All afternoon Jack and his cousins build castles out of Lego, then crash them down again. It's the best afternoon ever!

Hey Jack! The Crazy Cousins By Sally Rippin

Hey Jack! The Scary Solo By Sally Rippin

Hey Jack! The Winning Goal By Sally Rippin

Hey Jack! The Robot Blues By Sally Rippin

Hey Jack! The Worry Monsters By Sally Rippin

Hey Jack! The New Friend By Sally Rippin

Hey Jack! The Worst Sleepover By Sally Rippin

Hey Jack! The Circus Lesson By Sally Rippin

Hey Jack! The Bumpy Ride By Sally Rippin

Hey Jack! The Top Team By Sally Rippin

Hey Jack! The Playground Problem By Sally Rippin

Hey Jack! The Best Party Ever By Sally Rippin

Hey Jack! The Bravest Kid By Sally Rippin

Hey Jack! The Big Adventure By Sally Rippin

Hey Jack! The Toy Sale By Sally Rippin

Collect them all!